D0207377

About *The Thirteenth Gift*

While on assignment in Eastern Europe, Claire, a U.S. journalist, learns of a local legend. The deceptively simple story about "the thirteenth gift" has a profound effect on Claire, which soon transforms her marriage, her work, and the way she sees the world.

The Thirteenth Gift is both a cautionary tale and an inspirational fable as it shows a way through the perilous consequences of greed, arrogance, and abuse of power to an uplifted state of consciousness and community. *The Thirteenth Gift* invites readers to renew their sense of wonderment, which can lead to freedom from fear and to a greater experience of hope, beauty, and joy in daily life. Like the message of the award-winning book, *The Twelve Gifts of Birth,* this novella from Charlene Costanzo reminds readers to see the dignity that is inherent in themselves and others.

"A beautiful, engaging, and hopeful book.
It reminds us that every child is gifted."
—LINDA KAVELIN POPOV, CO-FOUNDER OF THE VIRTUES
PROJECT, AUTHOR OF *THE FAMILY VIRTUES GUIDE*

"A heartfelt story about the transformation
that is available to us all."
—SUSANNE M. ALEXANDER, CHARACTER SPECIALIST,
AUTHOR OF *PURE GOLD*

Also by Charlene Costanzo

The Twelve Gifts of Birth
A parenting classic and message for all ages

The Twelve Gifts in Marriage
Wisdom for all states of the relationship

The Twelve Gifts for Healing
For all the times when life hurts

The Thirteenth Gift

A NOVELLA OF HOPE FOR ALL TIMES

With love,

Charlene Costanzo

2/4/11

BY CHARLENE COSTANZO

FEATHERFEW™

FEATHERFEW™

Sedona, Arizona and Winter Garden, Florida

Cover design by Karen C. Heard
Text layout and design by 1106 Design
Printed in the United States of America
Distributed by Midwest Trade Books

Publisher's Cataloging-in-Publication
(Provided by Quality Books, Inc.)

Costanzo, Charlene.
   The thirteenth gift / by Charlene Costanzo.
   p. cm.
   ISBN-13: 978-1-891836-13-8
   ISBN-10: 1-891836-13-7
   ISBN-13: 978-1-891836-14-5 (e-book)
   ISBN-10: 1-891836-14-5 (e-book)
   1. Self-esteem—Fiction. 2. Self-acceptance—
   Fiction. 3. Hope—Fiction. 4. Equality—Fiction.
   5. Rocks—Fiction. 6. Legends. I. Title.
   PS3603.O867T45 2010   813'.6
                        QBI10-600219

Library of Congress Control Number: 2010941444
ISBN: 9781891836138

10 9 8 9 6 5 4 3 2 1

For Alexis and Anthony
and all the children of the world

"If a child is to keep alive his inborn sense of wonder, he needs the companionship of at least one adult who can share it, rediscovering with him the joy, excitement and mystery of the world we live in."

—RACHEL LOUISE CARSON

"Become like little children."

—Matthew 18:3

What is the attraction of stones?

Simple stones.

The type we come across on hiking trails, country roads, beaches, and city sidewalks.

What instinct urges us to stoop for them?

Hold them in pockets?

Save them in jars?

A little-known fable offers an explanation. According to this story, even the appeal of gem stones is rooted in something deeper than dazzle…something we are all trying to remember.

"This is the story of how we begin to remember."
—PAUL SIMON

Over a certain span of rugged hills in Eastern Europe, there rests a dense cloud. It has been there for as long as anyone in the low country can remember. Occasionally, the cloud thins, and for a moment, remnants of a crumbling castle can be glimpsed. Elders in the region tell a story about what happened long ago when a kingdom there was on the cusp of change. Most people consider it a pleasant yarn, spun by peasants. Few believe it's true. Yet, many say it *feels* true. Everyone, however, marvels at how travelers passing through this region learn of the legend in various, intriguing ways. Take Claire, for example.

ear midnight in a hotel room in Bratislava, Claire phoned home to Atlanta, Georgia. Hiding weariness, Claire feigned lighthearted laughter with her children, Maya and Michael, and said a quick good-night to her husband, Rick. She didn't tell her family that, having completed her writing assignment early, she'd be back in Atlanta in just two days, maybe even in less than 24 hours if she got lucky and a seat opened up on the 8 a.m. flight.

When Maya moaned, "Mommeee, *when* are you coming *home?*" Claire simply said, "Soon, sweetheart. Soon."

When Rick said, "We need to talk," Claire pretended she didn't hear and steered the conversation to an end. It was a weak connection, after all, the phone line. Well, the marriage, too, lately; but she'd work on that somehow, she thought, even while telling Rick she'd accepted yet another overseas assignment.

Yes, she'd be surprising them in more ways than one. Mommy is home early. Mommy has to leave again. Would Rick agree to it? She knew it was hard on him, being a single parent when she traveled, especially abroad. Thank goodness his programming job allowed him to work at home. *Just one more story this year,* Claire told herself.

Despite the strain and sacrifice for herself and her family, she felt compelled to show the plight of the hungry, abandoned, and abused children of the world. In the past six months, she'd reported from Mumbai, Baghdad, Bucharest, and now Bratislava. Next month she'd be closer to home at least, filing from Port-au-Prince, a short flight from Atlanta, with only one time-zone difference. *Cutting the call short was for the best,* she rationalized to the guilt nudging for her attention. *For now, the less time focused on my absence, the better it is for everyone. Besides, I don't want to risk spoiling the surprise!*

Before turning off the light, she checked with the concierge who advised her that securing a seat on the 8 a.m. flight looked unlikely.

"I understand," Claire replied. "At least I'm booked on the next day's flight. It's just that…" she paused, sighing.

"You are eager to get home, Madam. It is natural. If a seat opens during the night, I will phone you, of course. Is there anything else I can do for you now?"

Claire arranged to rent a car. If she couldn't fly home in the morning, she would at least escape the city for a few hours after an early breakfast. Driving aimlessly through the countryside was energizing for Claire, something she often did when she felt like her inner batteries needed recharging. Satisfied with her back-up plan and resolved to accept whatever the new day delivered, she set her cell phone's alarm to ring before dawn, turned off the light, and drifted into sleep.

The car was familiar, identical to a model she had previously rented, so she set off with ease. Soon, she was out of the confines of the city, meandering along autumn-dried acreage that stretched for miles in all directions. For Claire, riding through a vast expanse of land, in any season, had the same freeing effect as standing before the sea. She felt like a bird, as if she could spread wings and fly over the harvested farm fields where golden hops, barley, and wheat have grown for centuries. She rolled down the car's windows, inhaled the crisp air, and pressed on the gas pedal for high speed. Brisk wind whipped through her long, chestnut hair and lifted some of the heaviness that burdened her head and heart.

Cresting a hill, she braked in time to avoid a collision with a lone white goat. Claire mused about the solitary goat while she allowed the creature to complete his amble across the road without harm. *Where had it come from? Where was it going?* She recalled an interview with a Cherokee medicine woman whose answer to every question branched out from a central point like spokes from the hub of a wagon wheel. In the course of that rich discussion, Claire had learned about animal totems. *What was the symbolism of goats in one's life?* Claire tried hard to remember. *Surefootedness? A readiness for new heights? Cliffs to scale?* With the goat at a safe distance from the car, she resumed her journey at a prudent speed and traveled for almost an hour without incident until she approached a fork.

Claire slowed down and reached for the map lying on the seat beside her. She was unable to determine her location on the map while driving, even at a crawl. And so with her body aching for a stretch, she stopped before the juncture, turned off the motor, and stepped out of the car under a gnarled oak.

Mimicking the tree's branches, Claire reached toward the sky while arching her back. The view from under the canopy of spreading limbs stirred a childhood memory of rapture. For a moment, Claire was six years old again, wide-eyed and bursting with joy, sitting on the ground, resting her arms on the giant, exposed roots of the magnificent Moretan Bay fig tree in front of her aunt's house in Santa Monica.

That tree acted like an armchair for Claire, a place where she could rest, read, and muse. She could almost feel the cool earth beneath her legs and the hard trunk against her back. Claire smiled, remembering how she had imagined the great gray tree pulling up its wrinkly roots, becoming the mama elephant it resembled, and walking down the street with Claire on her back.

The increased flow of energy in her body triggered an inner prompting to renew her lapsed yoga practice. *Someday,* she responded to the nudge. *When I'm not so busy.* She twirled her wind-tangled hair into a coil at the nape of her neck and spread the map open on the front hood. Since both roads were unmarked, the map didn't help. Claire decided to simply continue on the wider, low road.

When she got back in the car, refreshed and ready to resume her excursion, turning the key failed to engage the engine. "Oh man," Claire sighed, while tapping her chest, a habit she'd developed in the early days of writing when she would concentrate so hard she'd forget to breathe. After five more failed attempts to restart the car, Claire tapped her chest again and inhaled deeply. *Okaaay. It is what it is.*

"Noooo problem," she said out loud, in the exhale. *I'll call the concierge. He'll call the rental agency and help will be here in no time.* She grabbed the phone from the drink holder and flipped it open. *No service.* With another deep breath, Claire tossed the phone into her bag, hoisted the bag onto her shoulder, and set off on foot toward the only structure in sight, a small stone house on the high road.

Muttering complaints, Claire kicked a stone in her path. When she encountered it again a few paces along, she gave it a swifter kick and lifted her head to watch it sail. After another punt, the stone became a companion on her trek to the house. Claire laughed to herself as she remembered this exact game from her childhood. As she did, the stone reflected a bright glint of sunlight. This time, when she reached it, she stooped, picked it up, and put it in her pocket.

A voice from behind startled her. Turning, Claire saw an elderly woman wearing a lime green babushka and a warm smile that lit her bright, blue eyes. The old woman repeated, *"Preco si zdvihol tento kamen?"*

"Rozumiem len trochll," Claire replied, while gesturing "little" with her forefinger and thumb. *I understand a little.*

"It is okay," the old woman said with a definitive nod. "We will talk English." Seeming to understand Claire's predicament, the old woman pointed to the stone house and invited Claire to use her phone. "You can call me Baba," the old woman told Claire as they trudged up the hill side-by-side. Although her crinkled skin, stooped posture, and wiry white hair poking out from under the scarf suggested an age of 90 or more, the old woman's voice and gait were surprisingly strong.

Claire followed the old woman into the one-room house and immediately felt welcomed by a fire crackling in the hearth. Baba led her directly to the phone—a square, black, rotary-style model—featured like an *objet d'art* on a crocheted doily atop a small wooden table.

Speaking with the concierge, Claire learned that help would most likely not arrive until late in the day. "I'm sorry, Madam," the concierge apologized. "I hope you can make the most of where you are right now."

Meanwhile, the old woman spooned cabbage soup into two bowls, set them on the table along with a basket of brown bread, and gave thanks for the food. While sharing the meal, Claire explained that she was a journalist, had filed her story, and would be returning home in a day or two. And she showed the old woman a photo of her husband and children.

"Ah," the old woman said, nodding. "Family." She began to rock forward and backward ever so slightly as she smiled into Claire's eyes. "Why did you pick up the stone?"

"What stone?"

"The one in your pocket."

Claire touched her pocket and remembered. "Oh, that. A habit, I guess. Sometimes I pick up stones. I've got a box of them at home. Most I've had since I was a kid."

"Hmmm."

When they finished eating, Baba took Claire's empty soup bowl, stacked it on top of her own, and set the bowls and spoons aside. "I know a story," she said.

"Oh? What type of story?" Claire asked.

"Maybe you could write it. Come look." Baba stood and walked to the window on the back wall. Claire followed. In the distance she saw a low mountain range shrouded with thick clouds.

"The clouds have been there as long as anyone can remember," the old woman said.

"Oh, a perpetual microclimate," Claire replied.

Ignoring Claire's meteorological conjecture, the old woman said, "Long ago, there was a kingdom there. After centuries of struggle, there came a time of opportunity. But instead of going forward, the kingdom went backward. When the trouble started, the birds flew away. Then, the deer, the wolves, the rabbits, all the animals, they roamed away. As if they knew. Little by little, the clouds gathered and settled. A darkness came and never left. I could tell you the story and you could write it."

"A folk legend," Claire said. "Sounds like a go
one, Baba," she added, tentatively. "But I don't
that kind of writing. I cover *news* stories."

"Yes, I know," the old woman shrugged. "Wh
you think are *true* stories."

They moved back to the table. The old woma
placed the bowls and spoons in the sink, added
log to the fire, and said, "You have time. Please
with me while I tell you the story. Relax and see
in your mind."

Warmed by the fire and the food, Claire close
her eyes and listened. As the burning wood crackle
in the hearth, she pictured the scene the woma
described for her.

"Back then, everyone took time," Baba sai
"Time to help a neighbor, greet a stranger, and noti
things like the smell of coming rain, bird song
and the changing light from dawn to dusk. A cli
walk surrounded the realm. Kinsfolk, common ar
gentry, strolled on it as often as weather and wo
permitted."

As Baba's voice flowed, Claire's imagination took flight. She saw the kingdom in her mind and settled in to learn what happened as the old woman continued the story.

fter years of longing, the king and queen of the realm were at last expecting a child. They rejoiced when, not one, but two babies were born, a boy and a girl. On the Naming Day there was a great celebration. All the kingdom came, from near and far, and gathered in the castle courtyard. According to custom, as trumpets blared, twelve godmothers arrived in the king's horse-drawn carriages to grant the royal gifts.

One by one each woman waved a hand over the cradles and chanted a word: *strength... beauty... courage... compassion... hope... joy... talent... imagination... reverence... wisdom... love... faith.* Music and fireworks filled the air as everyone celebrated until the night sky sparkled with stars.

"If only every child knew," one godmother whispered.

"Perhaps it is time they did," said another. "Let us visit Her Majesty in the morning."

The next day, choosing a peaceful mid-morning moment, while the queen hummed as the babies slumbered, the group of twelve women appeared at the nursery door.

"Godmothers," said the queen. "What brings you back so soon? Come see the children."

In hushed tones, the women marveled at the beauty and tenderness of the sleeping pair. "You have been greatly blessed, good queen," said a godmother.

"Indeed!" the queen replied. "The king and I are grateful. As we are for the gifts you have granted," she added.

"May the children grow to use them well," said another godmother.

"Amen," said the queen.

Sensing opportunity, the eldest godmother began, "Your Highness, for many years we have watched and waited. We come today with a truth to tell."

Curious, the queen led the godmothers to her guest chamber, sat, and asked, "What is this truth you have to tell?"

The youngest godmother stepped forward and glanced about, seeking support from the others. From their affirming nods she gained courage and declared, "Well, the truth is…the royal gifts belong to *all* children."

"Good woman, what are you saying?" asked the queen. "The *royal* gifts are granted only to *royal* children. Everyone knows that. That is why they are called the *royal* gifts. Why, it is as clear as day and night, as certain as the sun moving around the Earth."

"Things are not always as they appear," responded another godmother. "The truth is: we don't grant the gifts at all."

"What do you mean? Of course you do!"

The eldest godmother explained. "Your Highness, the gifts are from Our Maker. *All* children are born with them. We merely come forth and proclaim them."

The queen shook her head with disbelief.

The eldest godmother tried again. "The power, Your Majesty, is in *knowing* that you have the gifts," she said. "And in continuing to believe that they are yours to use."

"And…in using them," another godmother added. "And…and…there are more than twelve. And…"

Rising, the queen signaled dismissal, cutting off the godmothers' presentation. "I don't understand what you are saying, but I thank you for your visit."

The last godmother to exit turned and counseled, "If you look carefully, Your Highness, you *will* understand. All people have the gifts. With luck, some discover this and learn to use them well. Sadly, many never do. Look with keen eyes, good queen, and you will see that it is so."

Three years passed.

One day the eldest godmother appeared at a royal picnic, approached the queen, and asked, "Since we last met, have you seen that it is so?"

"Is what so?" the queen asked.

"The gifts," said the godmother.

"Oh yes, behold my children. Look at their joy. Already they are showing strength and talent."

"Indeed," observed the godmother. "But good queen, what gifts have you noticed in *others?*"

"Well, I have regarded a thing or two. The cook, for one…"

The queen paused and furrowed her brow. In her mind's eye she replayed a recent scene in the dining room with the cook. *How bold she was to serve mushroom strudel when I was expecting beef stew!*

"Yes, Your Highness, the stew you requested will follow," the little woman had said, with a proper bow. "But the mushrooms are so plentiful after the rain. And the chives, so alive. I picked them myself. Please try. If you wish, I will eat a morsel myself to assure you the mushrooms are safe."

What a savory meal that had been, thanks to her confidence, the queen thought while describing the incident. "Yes, I see courage in my cook," she said.

"And, without your cook's courage and talent, the mushrooms would have bloomed only in the soil instead of flourishing in the strudel too," the godmother said.

"I suppose so," the queen admitted.

The godmother watched and waited as the queen lost herself in thought before looking up to say, "And, Nanny, such imagination she has. I witnessed her showing the prince how an apple *cries* to be enjoyed when it is sliced, oozing sweet droplets of juice. 'Happy tears for the prince's health,' she calls them. My boy's appetite returned after an illness with the help of Nanny's whimsies."

"Your Highness. Yes. What may seem fanciful is often imagination at play, and what might look like impertinence could be true courage at work. Now, look for strength in others. And wisdom and hope. Look for *all* the gifts. You will see: what at first seemed far-fetched is *near*-fetched," said the godmother as she departed.

Four more years passed.

The king announced that he, along with his family, would be attending a royal wedding in a distant kingdom. In his absence, the king's power would be transferred temporarily to the regent.

On the night before the royal family's departure, the godmothers appeared at the queen's door. Again the eldest posed the question, "Have you yet seen the truth about the royal gifts?"

"I see the possibility, good women," nodded the queen. "Nearly every day I see at least one of the gifts in my subjects. Just today, the weaver who made this fabric..." she said, gesturing to her skirt, "showed me her compassion for all the creatures. While I was inspecting a new cloth she had delivered, a spider crept out from a fold. To my amazement, the weaver ushered the insect outdoors, through an opened window, instead of crushing it under her boot. Such reverence for life she has."

The godmothers sighed with a sense of accomplishment and hope.

"But, what is it that you expect from me?" asked the queen.

The godmothers proposed a kingdom-wide event in which the gifts would be proclaimed to all the people while celebrating the royal family's return.

"Oh my!" gasped the queen. "That is not in keeping with our customs. That would disrupt the order of things. It would confuse our people. And, my dear husband...oh, no, the king would not approve."

"Do not fear, good queen," said the eldest godmother. "There will be greater order. When everyone understands this truth, miracles will unfold." With a wave of her hand before the queen's face, the godmother produced a vision. "Behold," she said to the queen.

In front of the queen's eyes were babies' faces. Upon closer look, the queen saw that the babies were her own, as they were years earlier. Newborn infants. She watched with tender care and witnessed their eyes fluttering open for the first time.

Oh, that sweet moment, thought the queen. *I remember this. To have it again. Yes!* She surrendered all reserve and gazed with love into the purity of the prince and the princess who looked back at her with trust. Their eyes seemed to sparkle and speak, *Look, Mama.*

The queen watched with fascination as the faces of her own children changed into the faces of other children, first one, then another, each face shifting into the next baby face. In all those wide, innocent eyes the queen saw love and beauty, strength and courage, wisdom and compassion, a mysterious knowing.

It's true! At last she saw it, as the godmothers predicted on that long ago day. *The gifts do belong to all children!*

The succession of faces returned to the two most precious for her. Again she saw her own children, smiling. *Yes, Mama*, they spoke in her heart. *It is true.*

The faces then shimmered away and a large green heart came into view. The heart tilted to the left. Then it opened like a great yawn and transformed into a lush, verdant hill. The queen smelled the fragrance of grass and heard the faint sound of giggles. The laughter became louder and closer.

Over a vibrant stretch of land came hundreds of children—healthy and thriving, running toward her, squealing with delight. Multitudes of colorful butterflies—a wave of them—moved along with the children, dancing in the air that surrounded them. The queen stood in awe as the joy of the children glowed before her eyes. *I understand*, she thought. *There is nothing to fear. Instead, there is a wondrous transformation to welcome.* The vision then faded into a mist, and everyday reality came back to her tear-filled eyes.

"Great Goodness!" exclaimed the queen, crossing her hands over her heart. "The king must see this!"

"In time, he will," replied the godmother. "In his own way. But he must be prepared. On your journey, commencing tomorrow, help him see the gifts in others. Much is at stake."

Early the next morning, the royal entourage departed. The regent watched until the last of the royal traveling party disappeared over a far hill. "At last they are gone," he sneered, surveying the kingdom as if for the first time, and he smiled, for it was the first time that he was in charge, fully in charge, with no one to look over his shoulder. "Now, I can begin to set things right." He called a meeting with a few like-minded lords.

After grumbling about the king's relaxed rules, the growing freedoms enjoyed by the people, and having to share privileges with commoners, the band of men listened to the regent's plan to put strict controls in place. "It is a good plan, but we will need more time," said one of the lords.

"Ah, but I have a plan for that too," boasted the regent, chuckling aloud. "We will keep the family away as long as necessary," he hissed through tight lips while nodding to a sentry guarding the door.

After weeks of travel to the distant kingdom and a full week of wedding festivities, the royal family dozed in the plush pillows of their carriage as it rolled toward home. Suddenly, the lulling rumble of the wheels was disrupted by a loud CRACK! The coach lunged forward and sideways, jerking the family awake, and tossing the children out of their seats. Luckily, the prince and princess tumbled safely into the arms of their parents.

"What happened?" the king yelled as the queen soothed the children.

The driver's face poked through the curtain. "Oh, Your Highnesses...you are all unharmed? Thank goodness. Your Highness, it is the wheels. I don't understand it, but two are broken. I examined the carriages myself last night, as I always do. Everything appeared to be in good order. But somehow, several spokes on two of the wheels have snapped."

"Thankfully, no one is hurt," replied the queen, as the family alighted from the carriage.

Out of earshot of the queen and children, the king and his drivers discussed the problem. They had only one replacement wheel and lacked the proper tools to build another.

"I can understand one wheel breaking, but two? That is…unusual," mused one of the drivers.

"Highly unusual," the king said. He sent a servant to the nearest village to find another good wheel while the drivers put the spare one in place. Since the sun was already sinking low in the sky, the royal retinue set up camp for the night.

Early the next morning, a peasant carrying a sack ambled along the road. Nearing the royal encampment, he met up with the servant who was returning empty-handed after his search for a new wheel. Upon learning about the predicament, the peasant offered to help.

"Well, I'm no wheelwright," he said. "But I've made a few chairs. It seems to me a wheel is not so different from a rocking chair. Maybe I could fix the broken wheel. I've got my tools," he smiled, holding up his sack. "With your king's permission, I'd be happy to try."

The peasant was able to repair the wheel that very day. The king, pleased that their journey could resume with just a short delay, thanked the peasant by inviting him to dine with the royal family that evening.

After dinner the queen commented to the king on the day's events, "How fortunate that that peasant was able to help. His work showed talent and imagination, don't you think?"

The king nodded.

"And courage, too," the queen continued. "If he had been afraid to try, well…I don't know. I *do* know there is courage and strength in that young man."

"I suppose you are right," the king said. "Well, we have a long journey ahead of us. Let's sleep."

As their journey home continued, the royal party experienced many more mysterious challenges. Among them: tainted food and a missing horse. Fortunately, each hazard was overcome with the help of kind common folk who happened to be nearby and were always willing to offer assistance. In each case, the queen noticed the people's virtues and noted them to the king.

Yet another problem was encountered at the West Ridge Bridge. The advance horseman discovered that the wooden span was damaged. Instead of a complete sturdy pass over the river below, the bridge gaped open at the center.

"Can you repair the bridge?" the king asked his band of servants.

"Not safely enough to be tested by a crossing of a royal family, Your Highness."

The king ordered a courier to travel back to the realm they had visited and enlist the aid of bridge builders. "In the meantime, we will camp here and wait." When the first star appeared in the twilight sky, a young man passed on the trail in front of the royal campsite and learned about the broken bridge.

"It's a small trouble," said the youth, "Not a misfortune. If you wish, I can delay my journey and lead you to a safe crossing place in the morning." With the king's approval, the youth spent the night at the edge of the royal entourage, ready to help at first light.

Before falling asleep, the queen commented to the king, "Again we see virtue and gifts in a commoner, dear husband. During the past few days, strength, wisdom, and courage have been displayed before us. Do you see the compassion, joy, and talent in the young man eager to help us?"

"I recognize his kindness and lighthearted spirit. And, I trust that, tomorrow, he will prove his talent in showing us a safe crossing," said the king, smiling. "I've been wondering, woman, what is this new fancy of yours? You continually draw my attention to the good qualities in the commoners. I admire your appreciation for them. But, there seems to be a purpose behind this."

The queen opened the drape of the sleeper coach. A beam of moonlight shone on the king's face. Seeing his relaxed and receptive state, the queen raised her head from the pillows and turned on her side, toward the king. "It's true, dear husband. What you noticed...there is a purpose." The queen went on to tell the king about the godmothers' visits and their request to proclaim the gifts to all people.

"Proclaim the *royal* gifts to *everyone*?" questioned the king. "That would confuse the people and disrupt the order of things."

"That is just what I thought, at first," said the queen. "But I have come to believe this proclamation would bring widespread harmony and great advances to the kingdom. Just consider it, dear. That is all I am asking."

"As you wish. I will think about it. But don't count on this coming to pass. Good night and good dreams, my love."

"Good night and good dreams to you, Your Highness," the queen said with a kiss.

In the morning the king stirred from sleep, refreshed, renewed, and eager to make haste for home. The queen, already fully awake, asked the king, "Did you sleep well? Do you recall any dreams?"

"As a matter of fact, I had a magnificent dream," the king answered. "In the sky over our beloved land, an enormous rainbow arched across the sky. Its colors were more brilliant than any I have ever seen. I squinted at its brightness and more hues appeared. Twelve in all. And they sparkled like jewels."

"What do you make of this dream?"

"Surely it is a sign," said the king.

"Of what?" asked the queen.

"The unparalleled peace and prosperity that is possible for our kingdom."

"Oh, may it be so. Is that all?"

The king paused. "No. There is more. The rainbow is a sign for me to pay attention to the number twelve."

"Twelve? Perhaps, dear king, the Twelve Gifts?"

The king beamed a broad smile. "If the lad leads us across the river, I shall agree: we proclaim the gifts to all. It will be a sign to cross over from the old to the new."

At midmorning, the crossing place was found. The young commoner waded across a wide span of water, demonstrating its safety to the king and his entourage. "Don't try this next spring," cautioned the lad after wading back to assist the group. "It's low here for a short time only. We are in luck that the time is now."

"Thanks be to God!" the king shouted. Laughing, he removed his shoes and lifted the prince up onto his shoulders. "Hold on, son," the king bellowed. He chuckled to himself as his exaggerated steps sent splashes of water over both of them. "I wouldn't want you to get soaked."

The prince giggled all the way, pulling his father's hair to get even for the wet sprays he was getting. The queen and the princess rode comfortably as their coach rolled through the shallow span. Sunlight sparkled on the waves rippling out in the wake of the entourage's crossing.

Stepping up onto the opposite river bank, the king spotted a freshly discarded snake skin under a bush. He lifted it with a stick and showed it to the prince and princess.

"It is another sign," said the queen. "We *are* to shed our old ways!"

The king concurred with the queen. At the end of that day's journey, she wrote a letter to the godmothers, promising a grand party. *Yes,* she penned. *The king and I agree. It's time! Prepare to proclaim the Twelve Gifts to all! Begin as you see fit.* She stamped it with her seal and gave it to a courier, instructing him to deliver it directly to the godmothers.

At the halfway point, the queen's courier met a messenger sent by the regent to deliver a report to the king. The regent's messenger suggested shortening their journeys by simply exchanging mail and turning back. "It is a good opportunity for both of us to better serve, is it not?" asked the regent's messenger.

The queen's conveyor hesitated, acquiescing only after the regent's messenger assured that he knew exactly where to find the godmothers and would travel straight to them with honor.

An opportunity indeed! chortled the regent's messenger after the exchange of letters. He imagined the reward he might receive for intercepting the queen's missive as he hurried back to the regent instead of delivering the letter to the godmothers.

Upon reading the queen's letter, the regent raged. "Proclaim the Twelve Gifts to all? Preposterous! Ludicrous! Ridiculous! The commoners must remain...well, *common!* I will prevent this," he swore, tearing the letter into pieces. After tossing the shreds into the fireplace, he strutted to the balcony over the courtyard where many people had gathered.

"What word do we have from the king and queen?" yelled an innkeeper.

"They are going to be gone a spell longer," the regent stammered. "All is well. In fact, they say... they send word that...well, here is what they say," he said, taking a blank paper from his pocket. He pretended to read:

My good people. The queen and I will be traveling far and wide with our children for the foreseeable future. Listen to the regent and do whatever he tells you. You are in good hands.

"That is all. Now go about your business," he said, turning his back to the crowd.

Re-entering his chamber, he fumed, *Imagine making it so everyone thinks they have the same gifts as the royals. Ha! The lords, maybe. We are worthy. But the common folk? What grand ideas they would get. This proclamation will be stopped.*

First, he sent another letter to the king and queen, urging them to extend their journey. In it, he reasoned that, since all was well at home and they were already on the road, it would be wise to take the time to build goodwill with other realms and educate the children in the ways of the world.

Next, he called in his cronies. "Keep an eye on those godmothers. Better yet, find a way to discredit them," he said. "Make them look evil or stupid, perhaps both. And arrange for more hazards for our travelers. Steer them astray."

That was the day the birds flew away.

Among themselves, the people questioned the delayed return of the royal family. The regent heard of their murmurs and summoned all to the courtyard. Again he read a fake letter from the king:

While we are gone, I ask that you build a wall. All able-bodied men, women, and children shall gather stones and bring them to the cliff walk. Clear the fields. Gather all that you can. Fill in the walkway. Make it solid and tall. The wall will protect us for generations to come and be a magnificent sight.

When the regent saw that the people looked puzzled, he added, "We trust the judgment of our king, do we not? We must heed his wishes. I am sure he has good reasons for this wall. Let us begin right away. I will lead the way." And he stooped to gather a fistful of stones at his feet. "It will be easy. Everyone, fill your hands and your pockets, then follow me."

All the people then bent down and began to pick up stones. When their pockets and hands were full, they marched to the cliff walk and deposited the stones they had collected. "Do this every day," he instructed them. "In all your spare time. Make your king proud." And he returned to the castle, joined by his band of lords.

"What are you doing?" they asked.

"We must keep them busy," he said. "No more leisure time. They are thinking too much."

When a few people questioned the wisdom of filling in the cliff walk and spoke their concerns out loud in the crowd, they were secretly seized by the regent's men and brought to him. "I will confide in you," he said to them. "But you must not tell the others. More news has come from the king," he lied. "There is great danger beyond our realm. Threats to our kingdom."

As the regent expected, his fabricated news was shared with a few trusted friends, who spread the news to others. Soon, everyone whispered about "the great danger." And, in no time, the people increased their efforts to gather stones and to build the wall to protect their beloved kingdom. Day by day, the wall rose higher. Even the tallest men were no longer able to see beyond the kingdom. No longer was there time, or a place, for leisurely walks. Everyone got in the habit of looking down as they gathered more and more stones to thicken the wall. Even the children were becoming dispirited.

The deer roamed away.

More animals followed.

A sadness came over the land as a growing cluster of ominous gray clouds developed in the blue sky.

The godmothers watched with deep concern. "This offense must not continue," they said to themselves and one another. "Even nature is showing the gravity of this wounding."

In an effort to restore well-being to the kingdom, the godmothers sought an audience with the regent. Curious, he agreed to a brief one in his meeting room. But, when the women began to caution him, he turned his back to them, parted a drape, and stepped out onto his balcony. As he did, he inadvertently allowed a gust of wind to blow into the room, which stirred the soot in the fireplace and lifted a scrap of paper that had somehow escaped the flames. That little shred floated in the air and settled onto the open palm of the youngest godmother. On it, she recognized the queen's writing and the word "yes." The eleven other godmothers gathered close, each with focused attention. The remnant then grew around the edges, with enough words reappearing for them to understand the queen's intent. Not only did it say that there would be a grand proclamation upon their return but it gave the godmothers permission to begin to reveal the truth in any way they saw fit.

The godmothers immediately set to work. Watching for opportunities to point out evidence of the gifts, they began, each in her own way, to tell the people.

"I see you have the gift of courage," one godmother started to say to a young washerwoman who spoke up for a neighbor and stopped some gossip.

"It was nothing," said the woman, deflecting the praise while hurrying away.

To a burly man who had climbed a tree to replace a bird's nest onto a limb from which it had fallen, a godmother commented, "My heart is touched, good man."

"For when they return," he said. "The birds."

"Ah, yes, in another season. I applaud your hope, faith, and reverence, all the gifts that shine through you."

"You make too much of this," he said, minimizing the tribute and thwarting her effort to have him recognize the royal gifts in commoners.

One godmother observed the love she saw in a father who made a kite for his children. Although he acknowledged the love he felt, he denied having any other gifts, especially the "royal gifts."

An elderly woman with unsteady hands dropped a crock. With dismay, she watched it break into three pieces. After shaking her head with frustration, she carefully picked up each piece, spooned soil onto it, poked in a few seeds, and sprinkled water over each pottery planting. The godmother who saw this commented on the beauty, imagination, and faith of the act. But the old woman's self-criticism and grief over the broken crock hindered her ability to see and appreciate the blessing.

The godmothers recognized many more examples of the royal gifts in the ordinary lives of the people. Yet, in one way or another, most people denied their worthiness of the gifts. Many said, "Who, me? Oh no. The *royal* gifts are granted only to *royal* children. Everyone knows that. That is why they are called the *royal* gifts. Why, it is as clear as day and night, as certain as the sun moving around the Earth." Despite the people's initial resistance to seeing themselves as worthy, the godmothers persisted.

When the regent got word of what the godmothers were doing, he called for them. "You are forbidden to speak of these gifts," he ordered. "Do you understand?"

"We will do as you command. We will not speak of them," agreed the godmothers.

Immediately upon exiting his chamber, one godmother asked, "What shall we do?"

"I've got an idea," whispered another, gesturing for all the godmothers to follow her in silence. Outside the castle, she motioned again and led the eleven others to a secluded area in the courtyard.

"What is it?" implored the eldest. "Tell us your idea."

"We will abide by the regent's wishes and never *speak* of the gifts...but we will *sing* of them with the children!"

All the godmothers clapped and laughed with delight at this inventive solution. "Oh, surely this is evidence that you have the gift of imagination," the eldest lauded. And off they went.

Early the next morning, disguised as peasant women, the godmothers mingled with children doing their chores. First, everywhere they went, the godmothers hummed melodies. Then, they added words. The children heard and quickly learned.

One by one, on their way to fetch water, help in the fields, and meet up with friends, the children began to sing *I am strong, I've got joy,* and *I see beauty inside you and me.* Soon they were all singing the refrain: *We all have gifts to share, everyone everywhere.*

They were overheard by lords who rushed to report this new development to the regent. Upon learning of the children's singing, he fumed, stomped, kicked, and sputtered.

"The godmothers must have taught them these songs. We can't tolerate them any longer!" hollered the regent. "Those women must be banished! Summon them to me!"

In the blink of an eye, all twelve arrived and stood tall before him. "You wished to see us?" they asked.

"I have the power to banish you," growled the regent.

"Yes, you do," the godmothers said as one voice. "But that would be a grave mistake."

Ignoring their warning, the regent ordered, "I call upon that power now. Go! Leave this realm forever. Be gone before tomorrow's dawn."

With grief and concern for the kingdom, the women somberly left the castle and went straight to their hidden canyon. There, each closed her eyes, prayed in sacred silence, and listened for guidance. For a time no one spoke. Then, suddenly, many ideas rushed forth. But each was discarded. There was not enough time. Again they sat in silence.

"Wonder!" one of the godmothers suddenly exclaimed.

"What do you wonder, dear sister?" asked another.

"No, *wonder,* the thirteenth gift," the first woman answered. "And there is still this night's dream time."

"Oh…yes. *Wonder.*" All understood and quickly agreed on where to go and what to do.

That night, the plan unfolded as intended.

The regent and his cronies each experienced a long, restless, sleepless night of tormenting twitches, hiccups, aches, and indigestion, which kept them outside the dream realm.

Everyone else within the kingdom entered deep sleep and visited the dream realm together. In one common dream, everyone shared a vision about the return of the royal family. Trumpets blared and everyone gathered to welcome the king, the queen, the prince and princess, and their entourage—all except the regent and his cronies. At the height of the celebration, the godmothers proclaimed the gifts to all.

Even in the dream, at first the people were filled with disbelief. Each thought, *"Me? Gifted?"* But then, one by one, they felt the truth of it and sensed with awe the magnificent presents in themselves and others. Looking into one another's soul-filled eyes, a great hush came over the crowd. Then, everyone wept and laughed and danced and rejoiced.

The dream continued.

"Now, let's remove that silly wall!" declared the king, leading the way. At the wall, each person reached out and touched a stone, which then shimmered and sparkled. A great glimmering wave moved from stone to stone. The wall began to come apart. Some stones fell gently to the ground. Others floated back to the fields from where they had been taken. The clouds began to lift and separate.

Flocks of birds returned and flew in through the openings.

Like the stones, everything began to glisten and glow with rich color. The trees, the grass, the birds. The people. Everyone saw with eyes of *wonder*, the way a child sees for a time when he or she first comes to Earth. With a stone in hand, everyone saw the miracle of it all. The effects of kisses blown in the wind. The warmth that emanates from genuine smiles. The grace of prayers offered with gratitude. They saw and realized how all of creation breathes together as one in the heart of Love.

In the morning, rousing from sleep, everyone held a shimmering stone, a glowing reminder of the wondrous vision and of the Twelve Gifts within them. However, like the details of the dream, each stone faded and disappeared within moments, leaving behind a trace of hope and a glimmer of wonder.

As the people of the hilltop woke fully, a harsh reality stood before them. Each saw the thickening of clouds, felt the godmothers' absence, and sensed that the kingdom was doomed. Adults and children alike felt vulnerable in the face of the darkness gathering at their doorsteps. But guided by inner wisdom and inexplicable faith, they quickly packed and departed from the dying kingdom that very day. Some went north, some south, some east, and some west.

Only the regent and his band of lords stayed behind, sleeping that day away, after their fretful night of insomnia. They awoke confused, stumbling about, unable to find their way out of the darkness.

Soon, the royal family returned, but the clouds were too dense to penetrate. For a time they waited, hoping the clouds would lift. But the kingdom remained sealed, the castle beyond reach. The whole entourage wept, the loyal servants holding one another, as did the royal family.

"We must not despair," the queen finally said.

"No," agreed the king. "All is not lost." He gestured to the ground. "Look. In the many footprints and furrows leading outward in all directions, we see evidence that our fellow citizens and loved ones escaped this ruin."

He told the assemblage about his broadened understanding of the royal gifts. "Let us summon strength and faith. We must find a new way."

"Which we will, using our gifts," said the queen. "Each of us," she added, wrapping an arm around the prince and princess, who smiled up at her with love and courage.

It is believed that the royal family lived the rest of their days traveling the world, imitating the godmothers, revealing the truth about the Twelve Gifts to those who would listen. Here and there, they successfully planted seeds of understanding.

The godmothers continue to dwell in the dream realm, bringing messages about the Twelve Gifts to all who believe in miracles, as well as to non-believers.

"And that is the story," said Baba, pouring a cup of steaming tea for Claire, who shivered, more from the story than the cold.

"What happened to the kingdom is so...sad." Claire struggled to speak through a catch in her throat.

"Yes. That part of the story *is* sad," Baba admitted. "And, it is not the only time that an opportunity to leap forward has been missed. But, it is a hope-filled story. Come look," she said, rising from her chair, leading Claire back to the window with the view of the shrouded mountain. "The cloud is thinning. Someday it will lift. Despite the times in which we seem to go backward, we are always moving upward. All the children of the world *will* learn the truth about their noble inheritance. The godmothers are at work every night, nurturing the dream that passed on to everyone's children and to their children's children. The dream lives in you, Claire. That is why you picked up the stone. It is a touchstone for what you yearn to remember. The way you saw when you were born, with eyes of *wonder*."

"With the thirteenth gift," Claire smiled, wiping away a tear.

"Which leads to the fourteenth gift," said Baba, rising from her chair just as there was a knock at the door. Opening it, Baba greeted a driver from the rental agency, who urged Claire to hurry so that he could transport her to the city before the arrival of an approaching storm. Taking Baba's hands in her own, Claire thanked the old woman for her hospitality and the story.

"Tell the children," Baba reminded her.

As the car began to pull away, Claire opened the window and asked, "What is the fourteenth gift?"

"Peace, child," Baba replied with a smile. "Tell the children."

Claire nodded.

"And be ready for miracles," Claire faintly heard the old woman add after the window closed.

During the ride back to the city, the old woman's words echoed in Claire's mind. *Peace, child. Tell the children*, she heard again and again. *Be ready for miracles.*

*I*n the dark hotel room, the sleeping journalist reached for her ringing room phone. "Good news," the concierge said. "You get to go home today."

"Yeah, I know," Claire said, groggily. "Today's the day."

"Oh. You already got word? Okay. Well, I am glad there was a cancellation and you will get on today's flight. Have a good trip, Madam."

Cancellation? Claire sat up and grabbed her cell phone. The displayed time and date informed her that it was just five hours after she had spoken with her family. A full day had not passed? But…the drive in the country. Meeting the old woman. Hearing her story. It was all just a dream? It seemed so real.

Claire rose out of bed and padded to the closet where her slacks hung neatly draped over a wooden dowel. She felt the right pocket. It was there! The stone! She took it out and held it in her hand. How had it gotten into her pocket? Had she picked it up days earlier without realizing it? That must be it. The experience in the stone house with Baba was a dream. Just a dream. But as Claire remembered wisps of the dream within the dream and looked at the stone, for a second it sparkled with a glint of light, as if trying to convey a message. Releasing a deep breath, Claire squeezed the stone and laughed out loud. Baba! *In the dream realm! Nurturing!*

Claire hurriedly packed, checked out, and left for the airport. She reached the gate just in time. Settled into her last-minute seat—happily, a comfortable window seat in an exit row—Claire watched Earth's patchwork patterns appear as the plane lifted. A castle came into view. And what looked like the remnants of another. Over the public address system, a crew member invited passengers to see how many castles and ruins they could spot from the air in the next few minutes. "Although this region cannot claim to have the most impressive castles, the countries of Slovakia and the Czech

Republic have the highest concentration of castles in all of Europe."

That reference to castles triggered more memories of the dream. As more wisps and snatches of it came into her awareness, Claire noticed that, in the course of the past nine hours, since talking with her family at midnight, she felt young and renewed. The dream had healed something in her.

Soon the plane reached cruising altitude, and Claire retrieved her computer to begin typing the old woman's story. Near the aisle-side edge of her service tray, next to her laptop, sat the stone.

"Is that a magic stone?"

Claire looked up at the flight attendant who asked the question and smiled. "Sort of," she answered softly, in consideration of the sleeping young couple, newlyweds, in the seats next to hers.

"I've got one too," said the flight attendant, reaching into her pocket. She withdrew a stone and held it up for Claire to see. "It's got a story behind it."

"Really? I'd love to hear it," Claire whispered.

"Maybe later in the flight."

After completing her typing, Claire dozed like the newlyweds for the rest of the flight. During spans of semi-wakefulness, from behind closed eyelids, she viewed a changing future. She watched herself relinquish the Port-au-Prince assignment and remain at home for the rest of the year. A goat appeared. The goat in the road. Claire wondered more about what new direction it might symbolize, but saw only mist.

Upon exiting the plane, Claire saw the flight attendant and apologized. She was sorry to have missed the opportunity to hear the woman's story.

"I'll tell you this much," the flight attendant said, leaning in toward Claire, out of hearing range of the other crew members standing in the galley. "It restored my faith. It may have saved my life."

Curious, Claire stepped out of the flow of exiting passengers and deftly handed a business card to the attendant. Noticing her name badge, Claire said, "Sophia, I'm a writer. A story about a stone is not the usual material I seek, but please contact me if it feels important to you to share it. I think my work is about to change."

After clearing customs, claiming baggage, and enduring a 40-minute taxi ride, Claire arrived at her house. She tipped the driver generously and gleefully pulled her roller bags over a rare dusting of snow to the front door. Flurries swirled around her as she inserted her key. Turning the handle, she tilted her face to the sky and smiled at the wet, white flakes. Augie, the dog, was the first to greet her with barks and canine kisses.

"Mommee*eee*," the children screamed, running to her. "You're home!"

Rick stood leaning against the door jamb, arms crossed. Unlike the children, his eyes did not light up at the sight of her. She tilted her head and gave him her "I love you" expression, the look that used to bring a big smile to his face and stir an ardent embrace. He hesitated, then opened his arms to her. But instead of warmth, she felt a chill in his hug.

"What's wrong?" she whispered.

"Later," he said.

"How'd you do it, Mom?" asked Michael. "How did you get home *today*?"

Claire just smiled. After removing her coat and kicking off her shoes, she crossed the tiled entry and dropped down onto the living room carpeting. "Come," she said, patting the floor, gesturing for them to join her. Circled by her family, Claire explained why and how she got home early. And, she told them the story of *The Thirteenth Gift.*

When the kids were asleep, Rick turned off the TV in the family room and sat on an ottoman, distancing himself from Claire's position on the sofa.

"What's wrong?" Claire asked.

"You committed yourself to another overseas assignment. How could you do that without even consulting with me? I've had it, Claire. Your work always comes first."

"I hear you. In fact…"

"No, you don't hear," Rick interrupted. He stood up and paced. "Not really. You can't just say the words, Claire. You've got to show it. Withholding information is just as bad as lying. I'm tired of your disrespect and dishonesty. And, I'm tired of being

the father *and* the mother here. You can't go to Haiti, Claire, because I won't be here."

"What?"

"I've done a lot of thinking while you were gone. Although I love you, Claire—I do, and I love our kids—this is not working for me," Rick said. "As painful as it is, I'm moving out. I will be fully involved with the kids…as their *father*."

"I had no idea you were this upset, Rick. We have got to work this out. I know we can," Claire said. "Please sit down."

"I don't want to sit down."

"Let me tell you more about what happened for me in Slovakia and on the trip home. I am really seeing things differently," Claire said.

"Yeah, right," Rick uttered.

"Truly, Rick. I am sorry," Claire said. "It was wrong of me to accept the assignment, especially without discussing it with you."

"You say you value truth, you devote your writing to it, but you don't practice what you preach."

Claire heard the resistance and read it in his tense face and tight body language but pressed on, hoping that his mind would open and she could convince him to understand her point of view.

"Rick, about accepting the assignment...not telling you about it, not asking you...I..." Before she could finish her thought, Rick interrupted.

"You say you care about the well-being of children. What about your own? You are gone too much!"

"Yes. I know." A familiar tightness in her throat, chest, and abdomen stopped her from going on with her speech. She recognized the physical sensations that, in the past, had accompanied a desire to fix conflicts and control situations. *Truth, Claire,* she heard. *Open your heart and speak the truth.*

Startled by the inner directive, she paused, feeling led to remove her masks and armor. She prayed for courage. *Help.* In that letting-go moment, her defensiveness melted like mountain-top snow in April sunlight. Compassion, for herself and her husband, flowed like a clear running spring that follows the melting. Claire stood and reached for her husband's hand.

Sensing something, maybe the change she spoke of, maybe in the look in her eyes or the touch of her hand, Rick's resentment lessened. He accepted her gesture.

Guided by an invisible force, they walked together to the small circular table in the breakfast alcove and sat, face-to-face. The candle burning between them and the curved wall behind them fostered an atmosphere of warmth and intimacy.

Claire listened while Rick vented frustration and expressed concerns. She wanted to fully hear everything he was saying. Listening with care was a skill Claire used well with people she hardly knew during the course of an in-depth interview. Yet, it had been a long time since she had listened this way to Rick.

"I do hear you, Rick," Claire said, after he was through. Before saying more, she paused, allowing for silence to linger between them while they looked into each other's eyes.

"I agree that I have been gone too much," Claire spoke, at last. She wanted to share all that she'd been through. But she had no idea where to begin. She started with what seemed most important: what she learned.

"On the plane home, I saw that I placed too much value on work. I saw how I let it define me. Little by little I lost my true values; I lost my way."

Claire reached into her pocket, withdrew the stone, and held it on her opened palm near the light of the flickering candle. "This little stone reminded me of who I am."

She held out the stone for Rick to see.

"Who are you, Claire?"

Claire smiled. "I should say this stone is leading me to *remember* who I am. I don't yet know for sure, Rick. I do know that I'm not my job. This stone is asking me to go beneath all my roles to the place in me where...well...where the gifts are. The kingdom within."

Claire reached again for Rick's hand and opened his palm. "I already decided to pass on the

Port-au-Prince assignment. I am so sorry for trying to manipulate the situation and you. Please accept this stone, along with my apology, as a symbol of hope for us. I promise to be truthful and to rearrange my priorities. I love you, Rick."

She placed the stone in Rick's hand.

The flickering candle lit their faces while Rick sat without moving, without speaking, the stone centered on his opened palm. Claire breathed in the scent of the melting wax and waited, looking into Rick's eyes. The moment seemed eternal.

Rick curled his fingers around the stone. "I accept," he said with a smile that reached up into his eyes. "Welcome home, Claire."

ℰPILOGUE

𝓘n the days that followed, the children asked to hear it every night, the story of *The Thirteenth Gift*. And, every night, after the children were asleep, Claire and Rick talked more authentically than they had in years.

During that magical season, Claire and Rick moved through disillusionment to a renewal. Claire arranged for the Port-au-Prince research to be reassigned to another journalist and she stayed home with her family for the remainder of the year. In the new year, she reduced travel and shifted her focus. She no longer sought out evidence of what's wrong in the world. Examples of wonder and hope filled her writing and resulted in an award-winning series that showed how, despite grim poverty, children's lives are improving in Malawi, Tanzania, Madagascar, Nepal and Bangladesh.

The following spring, much to her surprise, Claire got this email message from Sophia, the flight attendant:

*Wonder is a gift that helps us open to all our
    other gifts.*
"Wisdom begins in wonder," said Socrates.
*According to Albert Einstein, wonder is the source
    of all true art and science.*
"Without it we are as good as dead," he said.
*"Everything, even darkness and silence, has wonder,"
    said Helen Keller.*
*"The more I wonder, the more I love,"
    said Alice Walker.*
Is wonder the gift that will ultimately save us?

It saved me. Want to hear my story?

✳ ✳ ✳

$\mathscr{A}$FTERWORD

"Remember. You must remember."
—CERVANTES

Dear Reader,

Thank you for reading this story.

One final thought…consider using an actual physical stone to help you remember and connect with the twelve gifts. Any simple stone will do; it can be rough or it can be polished. The point is, select one and let it help you keep in touch with *The Presence* and *the presents* of life in you.

A stone is a symbol of the wondrous oneness of all creation, as expressed in *The Thirteenth Gift* fable. A raw stone can represent how sometimes life seems harsh; the world appears ordinary; and we feel wonder-less. A polished stone can serve as a reminder that, no matter what appears on the surface, life's inherent gifts are always within us. Just as an unpolished stone's beauty is exposed and enhanced through a process of tumbling, the glorious reality of our gifts is brought forth, in part, as a result of the tumbles and stumbles we experience. You may wish to use *both* a raw and a polished stone and keep them side-by-side.

Since the conclusion of a one-year book tour from July 1999 through August 2000 throughout the United States, I have displayed polished stones in my house and carried a few in my handbag. My husband and I lived in a motor home and brought the message of *The Twelve Gifts of Birth* to schools, shelters, recovery centers, churches, prisons, hospitals, libraries, and bookstores. We called that journey: "The Polished Stone Tour."

The naming of the tour happened serendipitously. Before the tour, I had used polished stones to encourage some Arizona students to believe in their inner beauty and strength. When a third-grade boy from Tucson wrote, "Thank you for reminding me I'm not a plain old worthless rock. I'm like the shiny stone you gave me. I keep it in my pocket and touch it when I'm scared," I decided to offer the symbolic stones everywhere we went. So, when we moved from a 2,500 square-foot house in Phoenix into a 250 square-foot home on wheels—along with clothes, toiletries, food, cooking utensils, maps, business gear, and first aid supplies—we made room for thousands of stones.

Along the way, as the year passed, many children and adults said, like that third-grade student, that the little polished stone they received became a kind of "touchstone" for them, a visible and tactile reminder of their worthiness in times of doubt. And they shared stories. "Touchstone stories" I call them, expanding the word's meaning a bit.

According to dictionary definitions, a "touchstone" is a stone used to test the purity of gold and silver or, analogously, it is an example of the excellence or genuineness of something. Our stories of triumph and growth are examples of the excellence and genuineness of the gifts inherent in us. And, like polished stones, they can serve as reminders.

"The Polished Stone Tour" officially ended in August 2000, but in spirit it continues. In fact, my commitment to its intention deepened in September 2000 when I was diagnosed with advanced non-Hodgkin's lymphoma and was told, "There is no cure." The disease led me to examine my convictions and explore each gift more deeply than ever before. Looking for evidence of the gifts in others and in my own life has become a daily practice, a quest on which I invite you to join me.

If I meet you in person someday, I'll offer you a polished stone. In the meantime, I offer you a sampling of my touchstone stories. You can find them at my website, www.CharleneCostanzo.com. These collected memories, metaphors, quotes, and activities remind me to shift perspective and open myself up to life's gifts whenever fear, hurt, or limiting judgment has closed my heart. Just as one might hold an aquamarine stone in hand at a time that calls for tapping into courage, I hold a courage story in my mind and heart with the intention of having the example resonate and increase the flow of courage in me.

I hope that the touchstone stories you find at my website will spark recognitions of your own touchstone events. If you feel inclined to share a story or two about a time that you tapped into strength, beauty, courage, compassion, hope, joy, talent, imagination, reverence, wisdom, love, faith, wonder, or peace in a way that demonstrates the gifts' validity to you, please do. I welcome your insights and experiences. With your permission, I may post them on my website or use them in workshops and future books so that others can be enriched by your understandings.

May we all keep alive our inborn sense of wonder!

With love,
Charlene

$\mathscr{F}$OR $\mathscr{R}$EFLECTION AND $\mathscr{D}$ISCUSSION

1. When Claire feels depleted, one of the ways she renews herself is to drive through rural countryside and vast, open spaces. How do you respond when you recognize that you need renewal? How often do you consciously recharge your inner "battery"? In what ways do you do that? For more ideas, visit TheTwelveGifts.com.

2. At a symbolic fork in the road, Claire pauses to choose a route. Although she receives several clues from her body, mind, and emotions to change the path she is on, she decides to continue on the "low road." When her car fails to restart, she is forced to take action and a new direction. Recall a time when you stood at a "fork" in the

road of life. How did you choose a direction? What were the results and consequences?

3. Every day, we are faced with choices that require us to take either a "high road" or a "low road." Try paying close attention to them for just one day. Reflecting back on that day, what are some everyday choices that came up for you?

4. Consider the quote by Eleanor Roosevelt, *"In the long run we shape our lives and we shape ourselves. The process never ends until we die. And the choices we make are ultimately our own responsibility."* What choices shaped Claire's life and how did others she made reshape it? How does a choice gain power when responsibility is factored in?

5. When Claire re-enacts a game from her childhood, a sense of playfulness emerges as her inner child is accessed. When was the last time you experienced a state of innocence and playfulness? Think back to childhood. What simple

pleasures stirred wonderment in you? Think about sights, sounds and smells. What made you say, *Wow!* What stirs wonder in you now? Consider the quote by Ken Carey, *"When you remember the play that lifted your heart as a child, you will know the heart of God."*

6. Rachel Louise Carson said, *"If a child is to keep alive his inborn sense of wonder, he needs the companionship of at least one adult who can share it, rediscovering with him the joy, excitement and mystery of the world we live in."* Who has helped you protect and nurture your inborn sense of wonder? Can we renew our wonderment when it seems lost? What actions and techniques might help you do that?

7. Our inner gifts can be healing. To view a 4-minute film that conveys this message, visit TheTwelveGifts.com and see the *Twelve Gifts for Healing* video. After viewing the film, what is your response to this?

8. Have you ever had a dream that guided you or healed you in some way? In a way that feels most comfortable to you, share the details of that dream with others.

9. Apply Claire's dream to your life. If her dream were your dream, what is each character alerting you to do? Consider: Baba, the regent, the king and queen, the various commoners, the godmothers, the prince and princess. What choices are they asking you to consider?

10. The concierge says to Claire, "You are eager to get home. It is natural." Author Samuel Johnson takes this notion further in the quote, *"To be happy at home is the ultimate result of all ambition."* Too often many of us, like Claire, lose perspective; work then becomes more important than home, family, health, and/or our values. The concierge also says to Claire, "I hope you can make the most of where you are right now." What do these quotes suggest to you, in *your* life, right now?

11. A goat appears. It seems to Claire to be a symbol. She is open to intuition and to guidance in many forms. Have you had an encounter with any animal that seemed to bring you a message, encouraging you to pay attention?

12. When the plane lifts off, Claire sees patchwork patterns in the land and how things fit together like a beautiful quilt. Observing from a higher altitude allows us to see differently than when we are on the ground, in the midst of things. Similarly, with a higher perspective, we can see meaning and even blessings where once we saw only disturbance. Confucius alluded to this when he said, *"The gem cannot be polished without friction, nor man perfected without trials."* Recall a time when, with hindsight, you saw how what at first seemed to be a problem turned out to be a blessing.

13. Do we all have equal access to the spiritual gifts? In the book, when the commoners begin to hear that everyone possesses the "royal gifts," they say, "Who me?" How often do you deflect compliments and minimize your magnificence? Consider releasing limiting beliefs about yourself and practicing compassionate self-acceptance. Visit TheTwelveGifts.com website to access a helpful activity for this intention.

14. Claire asks Rick for forgiveness, and Rick is able to do that fairly easily. How does this quote from the Buddha frame his ability to do so? *"Holding on to anger is like grasping a hot coal with the intent of throwing it at someone else. You are the one who gets burned."* How do you feel when you hold on to anger versus when you forgive?

15. In what ways, if any, do you see present times reflecting what happened in the fable? How can this fable be used to inform the world now?

16. Rick asks, "Who are you, Claire?" Claire says she doesn't know for sure. Explore this for yourself. Answer the question, "Who are you?" Feel free to start with roles if that is what first comes forward for you. Then go deeper, listening for answers that come from your heart.

$\mathcal{A}$BOUT $\mathcal{C}$HARLENE

$\mathcal{C}$harlene Gorda Costanzo is an award-winning author, workshop facilitator, wife, mother of two adult daughters, and grandmother of twins. She holds a B.A. in Philosophy from St. Bonaventure University and an M.A. in Spiritual Psychology from the University of Santa Monica.

Originally from New Jersey, she has resided in New York, Texas, Arizona, and Florida. During a one-year book tour to launch *The Twelve Gifts of Birth*, Charlene and her husband enjoyed living in an RV in 48 of the 50 states.

The Twelve Gifts series of fables began in 1987 when Charlene wrote *The Twelve Gifts of Birth* as a life message for her own, then teenage, daughters. Twelve years later she published the book and discussed its message in schools, shelters, prisons, churches, and hospitals throughout the United States.

The Twelve Gifts for Healing was written while Charlene was in treatment for advanced non-Hodgkin's lymphoma in 2001. "Cancer led me to examine my convictions and look at these life gifts more deeply. Truly, they helped me heal," she says.

The Twelve Gifts in Marriage comes from the ups and downs, ebbs and flows, and hurts and healings that are a part of every long-term marriage.

To learn more about The Twelve Gifts and to contact Charlene, please visit CharleneCostanzo.com.

$\mathscr{A}$CKNOWLEDGEMENTS— $\mathscr{W}$ITH $\mathscr{G}$RATITUDE

$\mathscr{F}$or several years now, I have practiced a daily bedtime ritual. Before turning off the light, with paper and pen in hand, I list, in a steam-of-consciousness way, everything for which I am feeling grateful in the moment. I continue to be amazed at how this process stirs the flow of joy in me, which in turn, activates more gratitude. You probably have had this experience of gratitude precipitating joy and joy triggering gratitude.

It is with this same approach that I want to acknowledge the people, places, and experiences that have contributed to the birthing of this book about wonderment.

The Thirteenth Gift has been gestating since 1987, when I wrote *The Twelve Gifts of Birth*. Because this book has been in the process of becoming for so many years, it is unlikely that I will be able to name every person, place, and thing that has contributed to its development and publication. In fact, some influences are unconscious. I'm certain that this book has been shaped by early childhood experiences and unfinished business as well as by conscious thinking, choosing, and action steps.

Before I begin my stream-of-consciousness expression of gratitude, I apologize if you have walked a part of this journey with me and I have overlooked you in this listing. If I have not named you here, please know that, at many other times, you have been in my morning prayers and nightly thanksgiving.

I am grateful for Alexis and Anthony; Frank, Stephanie, and Krista; Steve and Phil and their families, too; *Ah, family*, as Baba said: all the Gordas and Costanzos, especially my own Mom and Dad and Keith; *Ah, friends*: Margaret and Mary Lu; Carolyn, Mary Anne, and Anka; Mary Ethel and *Hey, Patsy*; Glenice and Susan; Nancy G. and Willy;

Francesca, too; Sweet Spirits and Women of Grace; Kathy, Jen, Judy, and Sandra; Ellen, Chris, and Karen; Chris, Debi, and Koko; Cheryl, Angie, Patty; Laurel, Bernadette, Carol, Johnny...oh! entire class of '09; Ron, Mary, Alissa et al.; USM and USMers; Mary C.; *Hey, Jude;* Moretan Bay Fig trees on La Mesa; Sunshine Harbor, Bretton Woods, and Cherry Quay; LBI; Allegheny; Thunder Rocks; Panama Rocks; Sedona and Sanibel; SBU, Mother Seton and St. Elizabeth's schools; Brownies and Girl Scouts; Sister Carolyn; Bob and MM's car adventure in San Gimignano; lost on the way to Barea; cloud shrouded mountains, weeping willows, water stars, and lightening bugs; butterflies; Lawson Park; root beer ice pops, fresh cut grass, lilacs, forsythia, the first robin, harvest moons, geese migration; imagination; inspiration; The Polished Stone Tour and George; Minka and Bailey; Augie; Myah and Michael; seeing Slovakia; getting stopped in the Czech Republic; crossing into Poland; fresh baked bread, learning how to float; stones, shells, rainbows, fireworks, Linden library; 200 Summit;

Lake Chautauqua; 1106 Design, ABPA, Midpoint; John at B and T; Susanne and Doran; Gayle et al. at Changing Hands; Peg B. and Carole B.; Ling; Toppan Tom; Sylvia, Karen K.; all the marketing maniacs; Karen H., Wendy, Jill, Tina, and Cindy; Yoshi, Fido, Puma, and Panther; Myan and Pepper; and Josie, too; HC—all the folks I've worked with there; Rev. Kyra and Rev. Sandy; Lori, Peggy, Sheron, Carl, Michelle, Adele, Sylvia, Gene, Judy, Jim, all the Unity pray-ers; Derek and Rebecca; Miri and Joe; Di and Karen; Jan; Jenelle; Jayme; Mary Beth; Carla; Esther; Kelly; Melodie; Uschi; Martha; Andrea; Penny; Mazi; Kay; The Wellness Community; my favorite inspirational authors; Kripalu; The CASA; Susan Kay, Kasi, and Rob of All Gifts Music and *The Twelve Gifts of Birth* music; Deb; Joan; Julie; Joanne; Jane; Vikki; Terri; Trish and Paul; Dan and Linda; Val, Rose, Priscilla, and Barb; Mama Hawk; Paula Sue; Save the Children; friends and fans of The Twelve Gifts books; the shared stories. For all this and more, all the gifts from Our Maker. Thank you, God.

* * *

Special thanks to Susan Kay Wyatt, Kasi Peters, Rob Peters and All Gifts Music.

The lyrics: *I am strong, I've got joy, I see beauty inside you and me,* and *We all have gifts to share, everyone everywhere* are from *The Twelve Gifts of Birth* music CD, which is inspired by *The Twelve Gifts of Birth* book. Samples of this music can be heard at AllGiftsMusic.com.

$\mathcal{F}$EATHERFEW

$\mathcal{F}$eatherfew is one of the many wildflowers that grow in wastelands and barren soil. Despite inhospitable conditions, wildflowers thrive along roadsides, in vacant lots, even through sidewalk cracks. Humbly, perennially, without comfort, fine breeding or cultivation, they bring rich color, sweet fragrance and simple beauty into the world. And, they bring healing. Featherfew, in particular, is known for calming distress and lifting low spirits.

Like tenacious wildflowers, the gifts of the publisher, FEATHERFEW, are humbly designed to bring into the world a small measure of healing and joy. FEATHERFEW shares in the vision of a world growing in peace with an appreciation of the dignity of all people and the goodness of all creation.

FEATHERFEW is the original publisher of *The Twelve Gifts of Birth* (now published by HarperCollins) and the publisher of *The Thirteenth Gift*.

A portion of the profits from this book—and all books in the Twelve Gifts series—is donated to The Twelve Gifts of Birth Foundation which supports programs that prevent abuse and promote the well-being of children.